MILLIE
RIDE THE
RIVER

TROON HARRISON

MILLIE
RIDE THE
RIVER

TROON HARRISON

PENGUIN
CANADA

PENGUIN CANADA

Penguin Group (Canada), a division of Pearson Penguin Canada Inc.,
10 Alcorn Avenue, Toronto, Ontario M4V 3B2

Penguin Group (U.K.), 80 Strand, London WC2R 0RL, England
Penguin Group (U.S.), 375 Hudson Street, New York, New York 10014, U.S.A.
Penguin Group (Australia) Inc., 250 Camberwell Road, Camberwell, Victoria 3124, Australia
Penguin Group (Ireland), 25 St. Stephen's Green, Dublin 2, Ireland
Penguin Books India (P) Ltd, 11, Community Centre, Panchsheel Park, New Delhi – 110 017, India
Penguin Group (New Zealand), cnr Rosedale and Airborne Roads, Albany,
Auckland 1310, New Zealand
Penguin Books (South Africa) (Pty) Ltd, 24 Sturdee Avenue, Rosebank 2196, South Africa

Penguin Group, Registered Offices: 80 Strand, London WC2R 0RL, England

First published 2004

1 2 3 4 5 6 7 8 9 10   (WEB)

NATIONAL LIBRARY OF CANADA CATALOGUING IN PUBLICATION

Harrison, Troon, 1958–
Millie : ride the river / Troon Harrison.

(Our Canadian girl)
ISBN 0-14-331202-2

I. Title. II. Series.

PS8565.A6587M46   2003   jC813'.54   C2003-905023-8

Visit the Penguin Group (Canada) website at **www.penguin.ca**

For the First Nations people of Ontario,
in appreciation of their knowledge and skills

Canada

Newfoundland and Labrador

Quebec

P.E.I.

New Brunswick

Nova Scotia

 Marks the location of the story

MEET MILLIE

TODAY IT IS SO FAST and easy for us to travel every-
where by highway that it's hard to remember that
travel used to be very different. If you look at a map of
Canada, you'll see how many rivers and lakes there are.
Canada's Native people used these abundant waterways
to travel; the water provided their "roads." They were
skilled in building canoes from a variety of natural
materials. When European explorers and traders arrived
on the continent, the Native people taught them how
to canoe and where the water routes were. Early settlers
followed, penetrating into Ontario's wilderness by lake
and river. Waterways played a major role in the settle-
ment of Canada.

The story of ten-year-old Millie is set in 1914. At that
time, the waterways were used to ship grain and cattle,
to deliver supplies to isolated communities, to transport
mail, and to float logs from the forests down to the

sawmills. They were especially important in the area of Ontario known as the Kawarthas. *Kawartha* is an Ojibwa word that means "land of reflections." A canal system called the Trent-Severn Waterway—which still exists today—extended 241 miles from Lake Ontario to Georgian Bay and provided an all-water trade route that avoided the sometimes stormy Great Lakes. The canal system connected the Kawartha Lakes, and approximately 250 steamboats operated on it.

These steamboats carried city people in style to the summer cottages they were building on the shores of the lakes. The steamers ran excursions too, complete with bands and dancing. Regattas were popular, with canoe, sailing, and swimming races. The Kawartha Lakes might have seemed remote in 1914, but a busy social life existed there, with tourists and fishermen coming from many places for their summer holidays. Hotels and canoe clubs catered to the visitors.

In this story, Millie lives in the city of Toronto and is sent to the Kawarthas for her summer holidays. She travels there by train and steamboat. It's rather scary being all alone so far from home, but she looks forward to meeting her cousins, whose mother is an Ojibwa Indian. She also looks forward to fun and freedom on the lakes, a place where the rules governing girls' behaviour are not as restrictive as they are in the city.

"*I cannot tolerate any more of this* behaviour from Millicent," my mother said in the parlour below.

I sat very still on the top stair, listening, with my face pressed between the wooden banisters. They smelled of beeswax.

"Dinna fret," my father's voice replied soothingly. "She'll be a young lady soon enough."

"But yesterday there was that horrible—*incident*—in the alleyway. And today, she woke the baby with that wretched mouth organ," my mother complained.

I tucked my cotton nightgown around my toes and waited to hear what my father would suggest. I'd been sent to bed early, with bread and milk for supper. When my father came home from his work as chief engineer in a Toronto shipyard, I'd crept out to the landing to listen. I knew my mother was angry, although she didn't raise her voice. That would not have been ladylike.

Yesterday wasn't my fault, I wanted to call down the stairs. Tommy from next door and I had been playing with his yo-yo. It was only when a gang of boys from another street came by and threw stones that we defended ourselves by hurling sticks. If Bertha, our housekeeper, hadn't come outside just then my mother would never have heard about it. And today, how was I to know that Louisa May was sleeping when I balanced on the back fence and played my mouth organ? And now my mother had confiscated it!

Louisa May was a pain. First of all, she was a girl and I'd wanted a boy baby to arrive at our house, because boys were more fun. Then she was always either crying or asleep. *Hush, hush,* my mother and Bertha said to me all day long, all spring. The only time I wasn't supposed to be quiet was when I practised the piano every afternoon. I hated the piano!

I sighed. If only I was a boy, like Tommy, and could run through the streets chasing the iceman and the delivery wagons. Tommy's mother didn't expect *him* to sit still with his ankles crossed, embroidering straight lines of French knots. Tommy didn't have to learn to pour tea without spilling a drop or keep his clothes clean. If I was a boy, I wouldn't have to wear rag curlers in my hair, then stand perfectly still while my mother brushed my ringlets.

"Well, now, here's an idea," my father said in the parlour below. "Ye ken my brother Eddy?"

"Edward," said my mother, "that black sheep."

"He isn'a black sheep," my father said patiently. "He's a steady enough laddie. He and Mary might let Millie visit them up on the lakes for the summer. It would give ye a rest. What do ye think?"

"Oh, I don't know," said my mother. "She'd be running wild with those Indian cousins. She'd come home worse than ever."

"When she comes home, 'twill be time for school," said my father. "Let her have some fun while the weather is good. She's cooped up in the city."

"Perhaps you're right. I'll think it over," said my mother, sighing. Her dress swished as she moved to the parlour door. Quick as a cat, I crept along the hallway to my room.

Under my blanket, I lay with pounding heart. Cooped up! My father understood perfectly. Would he really send me north, out of Toronto with its clanging streetcars and bustling crowds? I had never met my cousins, but I knew that their mother was an Ojibwa Indian. Would they dress in deerskin? Would they live by a wilderness lake in a wigwam? Maybe if I could find where my mother had hidden the mouth organ, I could smuggle it with me . . . Thinking of this, I fell asleep.

Next morning, when I came down for breakfast, a letter lay in the silver tray by the door, waiting to be posted. It was addressed, in my mother's beautiful copperplate hand, to my uncle. I knew then that it was true: I was going to be sent away!

Several weeks later, my father and I rattled north on the plush green seats of a Grand Trunk Railway carriage. We'd been travelling since dawn when the milkman arrived. I'd fed his horse with sugar snatched from the dining table. My father had carried my grip, packed with dresses, and my mother and Bertha had waved goodbye from the front door of our big brick house.

Now hunger and excitement pinched my stomach. Outside the train window, a river glittered in the sun.

"It's the Otonabee River," my father said. "That's an Indian name."

"Is my Aunt Mary really an Indian?" I asked.

"Aye, she is. She's a good kind woman. Dinna go causing her trouble," warned my father, but his eyes twinkled above his beard.

"Your Uncle Eddy is a mate on the steamboats," said my father. "Water is like roads up here, ye ken. The steamboats take city folks to their summer homes and carry freight and mail."

I pressed my face to the window. On the far shore of the Otonabee, wooded hills lifted to a blue sky. I had never been so far from the city. Everything seemed clean and big.

My father pulled out his pocket watch. "One minute to noon," he said. "Right on schedule for Lakefield."

Soon we pulled into a station with a brown wooden building. While everyone was descending from the train with hampers and baggage, it was a busy place. My father and I climbed into a waiting democrat wagon.

"To the boat," Father told the driver, who chirruped to the horse. It was a short trip to the riverbank. The steamboat *Empress* rested there, gleaming white in the sun, with her gangplank down and a black-striped funnel chuffing smoke. On her deck, wooden slatted chairs were lined up ready for passengers. She was like a wonderful toy that I was going to float away on over the bright water. I hugged myself with excitement.

My father led the way towards a man at the foot of the gangplank.

"Eddy," he said.

When the man turned around, a huge grin lit up his weather-beaten face. "By the gosh!" he shouted. "My brother James! And this must be Millie!" His eyes, as bright blue as my father's, beamed at me.

I waited while Father and Uncle Eddy chatted, then jumped when the boat's whistle blasted.

"We'll sail with the tide," Uncle Eddy teased me.

My father handed over my grip and hugged me tightly. "You might want this," he said and slipped my mouth organ into my hand.

I followed Uncle Eddy up the gangplank and leaned against the rail on the top deck. My father waved, then began walking to the station. He had to catch the train home so that he could work the next morning. I watched his familiar figure disappear in the crowd of buggies and ladies' parasols. A lump blocked my throat, just for a minute. I was far from home in a strange place and away from my family for the first time.

Uncle Eddy's hand pressed my shoulder. "Do ye want to come and help me collect the fares, lass?" he asked, and I nodded. The boat's whistle echoed over the water. The crew cast off the ropes. With a tremor, the steamboat glided away, her bow pointing north between wooded shores.

After Uncle Eddy and I had collected all the passengers' fares, he took me into the wheelhouse.

"Cap'n," he said, "this is my niece Millicent MacCallum, who's come to visit."

"Welcome to the Kawarthas," the captain said. Then he explained, "That's the name for all the lakes joined together by river and canal in this part of the province. Newspapermen have called it 'the prettiest locality in Canada.' There's fine fishing here. Corn roasts and swimming and canoeing . . . Oh, yes, you'll have a great visit, young lady."

The river widened into a lake. A boom of logs floated past, bound for the sawmills. Cottages nestled along the shoreline, where water lilies bloomed.

"Now," said the captain, "we need more power in the engine room. Would you ring the bell?"

He pointed to the curved brass lever attached to a wire over his head. When I pulled it, he explained that I'd signalled the engineer for more power from the wood-burning boilers.

"How about a turn at the wheel?" he asked.

I gripped the polished wood tightly, and after a minute the captain let go. And there I was, steering the *Empress* up the lake while ladies reclined in deck chairs and the captain puffed on his White Owl cigar. I thought of Tommy; his eyes would widen with envy if he could see me.

I knew that I was going to have a wonderful summer—a grand adventure!

CHAPTER N.º 2

Later I went onto the deck. A group of chattering girls jostled by. One girl paused and leaned far over the rail. Her blond hair whipped across her face, and she reached up as if to smooth it back. Instead, with a quick shove, she tipped her straw hat over until the wind caught its brim. The hat whirled away. The girl gave a small shriek. Passengers exclaimed and pointed at the hat floating on the lake, but the girl winked at me.

"I hate hats!" she whispered. "Now I shan't have to wear it."

I clapped a hand over my laughter.

"I'm Edwina from Toronto," the girl said. "I'm going to church camp on Stony Lake with those other girls."

"Maybe I'll see you—" I began, but then Uncle Eddy called.

"Bye!" Edwina said, and I waved as I hurried along the deck to my uncle. He gestured ahead, and I saw the lake was narrowing into a river again.

"Young's Point, your summer home," my uncle said.

Eagerly I watched the village come into view. An iron bridge swung open to let the *Empress* through while children watched. I wondered if any of them were my cousins and if they would be happy to meet me.

Beyond the bridge was a lock, which Uncle Eddy explained was for raising and lowering the water level between the lake and river. After the *Empress* sailed into the lock, the gates would swing shut and water would pour in to fill it. Up, up the *Empress* would float until her funnel, then her upper deck, were above the lock wall. Finally, the second gate would open and the *Empress* would sail out to continue north.

Before that happened, though, it was time for me to get off.

"Ye just walk along the road to Young's store and buy yourself some candy," said Uncle Eddy, slipping me a penny. "They'll tell ye in there how to find your Aunt Mary. I'll see ye this evening after work."

I balanced down the gangplank. Around me people greeted one another, laughing and chatting. For the second time, I felt all alone. I set out along the dusty road to the general store, where the lady behind the counter explained how to find my aunt. Soon I was walking south past green and white cottages. The lake shone through the pine trees.

My mother would have been horrified to see me walking alone in a strange place. "This is not suitable," she would have said. I smiled to myself, but I almost wished she was with me.

"Nine . . . ten . . . eleven," I said aloud, counting the shoreline houses past the stone church. Here was where my cousins lived—not in a wigwam, but in a wooden house with a screened verandah. Shyly I knocked on the back door. It was opened by a lady in a faded cotton dress. Her black hair hung over her shoulders in fat braids, and her dark eyes looked kind.

"Aunt Mary?" I asked politely. "I'm your niece, Millicent MacCallum."

She bent and gave me a gentle hug and then, in a soft voice, she invited me in. I drank lemonade in the hot kitchen while she made blueberry pies. She listened silently while I described my journey.

"Feather and Matthew, your cousins, are fishing," Aunt Mary said, sliding the pies into the wood stove. "Do you want to look for them?"

"How old are they?" I asked.

"Feather is ten, the same as you. Matthew is thirteen."

I nodded and went out, crossing the yard to the lakeshore. I shielded my eyes, but couldn't see any children fishing, just one old man rowing past. I lay in the hammock in the shade and soon fell asleep.

"Who's this?" asked a voice.

I opened my eyes. Thin black braids swung over me, framing a brown face.

"Feather?" I asked, and the girl nodded.

"I'm your cousin Millie," I explained, trying to sit up while the hammock rocked. "I'm here for the summer."

Feather nodded, as calm as her mother. "It's suppertime," she said.

Matthew waited with a string of fish. He watched silently as the hammock flipped, pitching me headfirst onto the grass. I sprang up, but my cousins didn't laugh; they just stared with those dark eyes that seemed to know all kinds of things I didn't.

I hurried behind them to the house, where my aunt was setting food onto a weathered table on the verandah. Uncle Eddy joined us, his arms still wet from the pump, and gave me a wink. I felt better now that he was home because his blue eyes reminded me of Father's, helping to make me feel less alone in a strange place.

There was no cloth on the table. Aunt Mary didn't tell Feather to change her dress, and she didn't tell Uncle Eddy to comb his hair—even though it stood up in wild curls like Father's did before he smoothed it flat with pomade. No one said anything when Matthew reached under my nose for a dish of beans or when Feather used her fingers to lift the spine from her fish. Mother would have been horrified!

I was going to love it here. I would plait my ringlets into braids and wear only my oldest dress; I'd take off my white socks and buckled

Matthew waited with a string of fish. He watched silently as the hammock flipped, pitching me headfirst onto the grass.

shoes and go barefoot like my cousins. I would do everything I wasn't allowed to at home.

After supper, Uncle Eddy trimmed the lamp wicks. My cousins and I wandered to the water and sat on the warm boards of the dock. Ripples were pink in the sunset.

"Do you want to go for a paddle?" asked Feather. She pointed to the canoes tied to the dock. They were made of birchbark and thin strips of curved wood. They looked too flimsy to hold me safely above the deep water.

"I don't know how," I said.

Feather stared. "Everyone here knows how to paddle a canoe."

"It's different in the city," Matthew said, whittling a piece of wood.

I felt dumb; I wanted my cousins to like and admire me.

"My mother is a lady from a rich family in England," I blurted. "Her father owns racehorses that win golden cups. Fifteen servants work in his house."

My cousins didn't gasp and make their eyes round, the way city children did when I told them these facts. They remained silent while water slapped the dock.

Then Feather said, "My mother is the great-niece of Chief Handsome Jack."

"Who's he?" I asked.

"He owned the hunting rights north of here," Feather said. "He was the father of Polly Cow, who died of a broken heart."

"What do you mean?"

"It was like this," Feather said, curling her legs under her. "Polly Cow was sixteen and very beautiful. She had eyes as dark as a doe's and hair as smooth as moonlight on water. When she sang, her voice was like wind in the trees. She fell in love with a man from another tribe, but her father forbade them to meet. He moved Polly away to another lake so that she couldn't see her lover. But Polly sickened with a fever. It was her heart breaking. And when she died, they lit torches and made a procession with canoes. They came down this lake, past this shore."

"Our dock wasn't here then," said Matthew.

"Their mourning cries echoed over the water. They paddled to Polly Cow Island—"

"Only it wasn't called that then," Matthew interrupted again.

"They put out their torches. In darkness and silence they buried her. Her father, Chief Handsome Jack, laid a tin cup on her grave."

"What for?" I asked.

"So her spirit could go and drink from the water's edge," said Feather. "Her spirit lives on the island."

Feather's voice had sunk to a whisper and her dark eyes were solemn. A chill ran over my arms and down my neck.

"I don't believe you," I said. "Her spirit would be in heaven."

But then, I thought, maybe it wouldn't be there, because my mother once said that the Indians hadn't known anything about God and heaven until the white preachers saved them. So if Polly Cow's spirit wasn't in heaven, where was it?

Suddenly, a wild laughing cry shivered over the water. I jumped and then rubbed my arms to cover my fright.

"What was that?" I asked as the echoes died.

"It was Polly Cow's spirit," said Feather.

I stared at the dark pines whispering on the shore. "I'm not afraid of spirits," I said.

I looked at Matthew, hoping he'd grin the way Tommy did when I said I wasn't afraid to steal an apple from the cart of Luigi, the Italian fruit seller. But Matthew just kept whittling.

"I'm not afraid of anything," I said louder.

"Then paddle over to Polly Cow Island and call her name three times," dared Feather.

"I don't know where it is," I said.

"It's right there."

I looked where Feather pointed, down the lake. The island was like the back of a turtle floating on the pink water. Feather untied a canoe.

"It's easy to paddle," she said softly. "Are you afraid?"

"No." I climbed into the rocking canoe. At any minute it would flip over, like the hammock. I hadn't told Feather that I couldn't swim. When she gave the bow a push, the canoe drifted away from the dock. I dipped the paddle into the water and the canoe skimmed forward.

I paddled without looking back. The canoe didn't go in a straight line. I shifted the paddle from hand to hand, trying to make the canoe go where I wanted. What was the matter with it? My cousins' eyes burned between my shoulders. They were probably snickering as I twirled in circles.

The air was silent. It was never this quiet in the city. I shivered. Around the island, the water was inky. Tree limbs brushed the surface. Before I could stop it, the canoe slid beneath them and bumped into the shore.

"Polly Cow!" I whispered. My stomach heaved, my hands clenched the paddle. I couldn't breathe.

"Polly Cow!" I squeaked. My cousins would never hear me from the dock. My mouth was dry as a dog's old bone.

Wind sighed through the trees, chasing the shadows. I swallowed my terror. Was that shadow a woman coming to the water with a tin cup in one hand? Was that pale glimmer a birch branch—or an arm?

Crack! What made that twig snap?

"Polly Cow!" I screamed and shoved at the bank with all my might. The canoe scooted backward. I dug the paddle into the water and the canoe shot against the bank again. Twigs tangled in my hair like bony fingers, tugging. I screamed and struggled. Pine cones dropped onto my shoulders like fingers tapping. I shoved the canoe off again. The bow swung into the darkening lake, and I tried to turn it towards the dim shore. Gasping, I looked over my shoulder.

The island was a dark, mysterious bump again. I couldn't tell if anything watched me leave.

Finally I got the canoe turned around. I strained my eyes, trying to see the dock. It was hard to tell which house to steer towards; everything looked different from out here. The sky faded as the pale moon rose above the eastern treetops. Panting, I moved the canoe forward on a zigzag course. I could see the dock now. My cousins were dark blobs.

"Did you hear me?" I tried to call, but my voice croaked.

Suddenly, through the still air, came that eerie cry again. It was the ghost of Polly Cow calling for her lover as she died of a fever. Sweat broke out on my hands. Hair stood up on my neck. The canoe shot towards the dock and I began to stand up. I was going to scramble forward, leap onto the dock, run to the house.

The canoe tipped.

I plunged headfirst into choking darkness.

My arms thrashed. My legs kicked. Bright lights exploded in my head. My mouth gasped for air as I surfaced. Something banged against

25

my head. I yelled and water poured into my mouth. I went under, lungs burning.

I would never see my mother again, or my father, or Louisa May's button nose.

Suddenly something grabbed my shoulders and hefted me out. Water streamed into my stinging eyes. "Don't struggle," said Matthew, and he hauled me onto the dock. My teeth chattered with shock and Feather looked horrified. I retched up fishy water.

"You should have said you can't swim," Feather said, sounding friendly for the first time. She picked weed off the starched white collar of my dress.

In the water, Matthew stood neck deep and tipped the canoe over and bailed it out with a can. "Take Millie into the house," he said.

Feather dragged me towards the verandah steps. "That noise?" she panted. "It was only a bird called a loon. I'm sorry I tricked you."

The next morning when I awoke, I noticed the quiet. No hooves clattered past. No vegetable seller cried his wares. I slipped off the tick mattress I'd shared with Feather and padded to the window. The lake looked inviting and innocent this morning—very different from the lake that had terrified me the night before. While I watched, Matthew ran across the dewy grass and dove off the dock, making a fountain of spray. Maybe if I went down he'd teach me to swim too! After all, he had helped me last night.

The problem was, I had no bathing costume. Maybe I could just wear a petticoat? In my imagination, my mother frowned; perhaps I was too old to swim in a petticoat. Well, maybe I could swim in my oldest dress? When I lifted it from my grip, it didn't look as old as I'd hoped. Compared with what Feather had worn the day before, it looked quite clean and new: blue with a ruffle at the hem and lace at the wrists. Maybe if I tore the ruffle and the lace off? I broke the stitches with my teeth and pulled; the ruffle came away with a tearing sound. I bit off dangling threads, then set to work on the lace.

Feather's eyes opened. She watched me from the bed without saying anything.

"I'm using it to swim," I announced boldly, hoping she wouldn't laugh at me or say anything about what had happened with the canoe.

"I think we have to do the window screens this morning," was her reply.

"Do what to them?"

"Paint them with lamp black and linseed oil so they don't rust. It's our chore for this morning."

"Oh." I bit threads off in disappointed silence. It didn't seem fair that even here—so far from the bustling city—we had chores to do. Sun sparkled on grass and water, and I wanted to be outside running with bare feet for the first time I could remember.

But Feather was right. After breakfast Aunt Mary sent Matthew out in the rowing punt to collect driftwood for kindling, and she told Feather and me that it was time to paint the screens. She lifted them, inside their wooden frames, from the windows. We laid all the screens flat on the grass. Then Aunt Mary brought us two brushes and a can filled with an oily black liquid. The brushes soaked it up. We swept it to and fro over the screens, coating their wire mesh.

Feather didn't say much while we worked. I wondered whether she was always quiet or whether she thought I was too stupid to talk to because I couldn't paddle and couldn't swim and had arrived wearing ruffles and hair ribbons. Maybe she thought I was a dumb city person— but I wanted to show her that I wasn't like that. I wished she knew things about me: how I could balance along the fence at home; how I could throw a rock straight; how I really had stolen the apple from the back of Luigi's fruit wagon for a dare (but I paid for it later with my allowance).

When all the screens were painted on one side, we flipped them over and painted the other side. I dribbled the mixture of lamp black and oil over my bare toes by mistake, but I didn't care. No bustling Bertha was going to scold me about making extra work for her heating bath water. Here I could be as dirty as I chose. I smiled to myself.

It was while Feather was using the facilities (only she called it "the outhouse") that I had my idea. When the screens were finished, Feather and I could use the leftover oil mixture for a game. Maybe Matthew would play, too. We'd find some old flour bags and paint them with skulls and crossbones, and we'd paint black marks on our cheeks and be pirates. I wondered if Aunt Mary had a jewel box like my mother's. We could borrow golden earrings and make swords from sticks . . . this was a great idea! I couldn't wait to explain it to Feather.

I grabbed the can of lamp-black mixture and ran towards where the outhouse leaned at an angle in a grove of poplar trees. I sped around the corner of the verandah.

Whump!

Something hit my head, my ribs. I fell backwards, the can spinning from my hands. Air whooshed from my lungs. My head hurt.

When I opened my eyes, Feather was climbing to her feet. All down the front of her dress was a black spreading, dribbling stain. The empty can lay on the path between us.

Feather's eyes were snapping stars. "You've ruined my dress!" she hissed. "Are you happy now? You've got your own back for the loon trick last night!"

"I wasn't trying to get—"

"*You* might have so many dresses that you can rip them up, but *I* don't!" she said. "This was my favourite and it's stained forever!"

For the first time I noticed the dress's pretty lavender colour and pearly buttons. The stain of black continued spreading as it soaked into the fabric. I noticed that Feather was even wearing a purple hair ribbon, and that its trailing ends were tipped with black.

"But, Feather, listen. *Please!* I had an idea for a game and I—" She stuck her nose in the air as if I smelled bad, and stepped daintily around where I sprawled in the path. Then she stomped up the verandah steps and disappeared inside, clutching her dress with both hands.

I felt terrible. I picked up the empty can and set it near the screens. Then I wandered to the dock and dangled my toes in the water. I wondered whether Aunt Mary would punish Feather or whether she'd punish me. Perhaps I'd be sent back to the city. How could I convince Feather that I hadn't ruined her dress deliberately,

When I opened my eyes,
Feather was climbing to her feet.
All down the front of her
dress was a black spreading,
dribbling stain.

that everything had been an accident because we had both run around the same corner at the same moment?

I wished I knew how to paddle the canoe or to swim. Instead I had to content myself with wading along the shallow edge of the lake, feeling the grit poke my soft, pale feet. I bent to watch something shrimplike scuttle beneath a rock. Once I heard the strange bird, the loon, crying. In the daylight its call sounded like laughter.

Feather came out and walked silently along the dock on her bare feet. Against her knees, a dress of worn deerskin flapped softly. Suddenly I understood that she'd worn her lavender cotton dress to be like me in my city clothes—and I'd ruined it. I wanted to explain myself again, but Feather didn't look in my direction. She carried a bait can full of worms in one hand and a lunch pail in the other. After untying her canoe, she stepped into it so neatly that it hardly moved and picked up her paddle. Quickly, she paddled away with the canoe skimming in a straight line. When she was out of sight around the wooded point, I sneaked back indoors. My bare feet were silent on the plank floors as I crossed the front room with its stone fireplace and watercolour sketches of sailing regattas. From my grip, in the bedroom loft I shared with Feather, I fetched my mouth organ. Tiptoeing back through the house, I wondered where Aunt Mary was.

I stuck my head around the kitchen door and there was my aunt, swinging an axe in the back yard. *Swish, thunk. Swish, thunk.* My eyes widened with amazement. I had never seen a woman use an axe before. Aunt Mary's arms soared magnificently through the air, and the shining blade severed each block of wood perfectly in half. I crept away before she noticed me spying.

I took my mouth organ to the end of the dock to play, but it seemed to make lonely sounds. After a few minutes, I stopped and lay on the crooked boards, feeling the warm sun on my face.

When I returned home, my mother would scold me for being so tanned and for not wearing my hat. Her complexion was always white, winter and summer. Her beautiful blond hair was always neat in its bun. Her neck smelled of rose-water, her little heels clicked on the polished floors. When I was sick in bed with measles, her hands smoothed my hair back from my hot face, while she read stories to me in her gentle voice.

My throat ached.

I wondered what Bertha was doing: whether she was making my favourite raisin pudding for lunch or was in the garden beating the rugs on the line. Sometimes she let me beat them too, and I'd pretend I was being attacked by wild elephants. Maybe Louisa May was waking from her morning nap, and cooing and waving chubby fists in the air. Sometimes when she was like that, I'd hold her and talk to her. She was all right then, even if she wasn't a boy.

Distant voices broke into my thoughts, and I sat up to look around. A sailing boat was gliding past on the blue lake, with two ladies on board. As I watched, they turned the bow into the wind and the boat rocked to a stop. One of the ladies—she looked a little like my mother with blond hair in a bun—stood up, laughing. She wore a navy blue costume and a little hat like a pancake. Suddenly, neat and swift as a bird, she dove over the stern of the boat.

I stared the same way I'd stared at Aunt Mary chopping wood. I'd never seen women out alone in a boat, diving and swimming, before. As I watched, the woman swam lazy circles around the boat while the breeze played in the sail. At last, she hauled herself aboard and the woman at the tiller swung the bow around. The sail filled with wind, and the boat shot across the lake, leaning over as a sudden gust reached it. The women's laughter carried across the water. They looked as if they were having so much fun together . . .

I began to play my mouth organ with all my might, sucking and blowing, air whooshing through me—so that I had no breath left over to cry with.

CHAPTER N° 4

"*Sometimes I hate being a girl,*" *I said,*
scuffing my shoes along the road. My feet were
too sore to go bare. I'd have to toughen them up
gradually until they were like Feather's.

Aunt Mary gave me a puzzled look.

"Why do you hate being a girl?" asked Feather.

I frowned, watching my shoes move from
sunlight into shadow. We were walking to Young's
Point to buy supplies.

"Because . . . my mother wants me to be a lady
like her, and stay indoors and embroider samplers

and play the piano. But I like it outside better. I like *doing* things."

"Well, I do things outside and I'm a girl," said Feather.

"I guess—it's different here," I said. "Maybe here it's okay for ladies to do things outside."

If my mother lived here, would she chop wood and gut fish? And if she did, would she still be a lady? Life was puzzling.

I jumped to pull a green apple from a wild tree beside the road. It was warm and smooth in my hand. When I bit it, the juice was sharp as lemons.

"What do you think, Aunt Mary?" I asked.

My aunt strode along in silence. She never rushed her words the way I did. Her words came out calm and thoughtful. "I think we'll visit Mrs. O'Neill," she replied.

I raised my eyebrows at Feather but she shrugged. She didn't know what this answer meant either.

In the general store, while Aunt Mary shopped, Feather and I explored. We were closer to being friends now, since I'd written her a note explaining the accident with the lamp black. She hadn't exactly said she'd forgiven me, but in the three days since, she'd stopped ignoring me. And neither of us was punished. Now we peeped into barrels of beans and demerara sugar, and I described the milliner's shop my mother frequented in Toronto, where you could buy taffeta, watered silk, muslin, and Brussels lace.

Aunt Mary packed the supplies into a woven carrier that she slung over her back. She was strong! At home, my father always lifted anything heavy. I thought that maybe Aunt Mary was almost as strong as he was. Perhaps it was because she was an Indian.

"Now to Mrs. O'Neill's," she told us. We followed her up the road, across a meadow, through a band of cedar trees, over a creek on a board plank, up a hill. At the top, a log cabin with red curtains stood amongst birch trees. My aunt rapped at the door. When Mrs. O'Neill opened it, her deep wrinkles creased with a smile. "Mary and Feather," said her clear voice. "And who is this?"

"This is Millie from Toronto. She's come to see how a woman lives in the wilderness," said my aunt.

Mrs. O'Neill laughed a chiming note. "Has she, begorra? Then she'll be after needing the grand tour." And she stepped outside where the sun shone on her short silver hair.

She led me to the pen she had built from sapling poplars, trimming them with her axe. Inside the pen stood three nanny goats and a billy with a brown beard. Mrs. O'Neill sent Feather for the milking pail, and she sat on a three-legged stool and demonstrated how to milk a goat. Then she made me try; the goat smelled funny and I couldn't get any milk from its warm, hairy teats. Then Mrs. O'Neill showed us the root cellar she'd dug herself by hand. Although she was not an Indian, I thought she was strong, too! In Mrs. O'Neill's garden, the sweet corn she'd planted was tall. On the west wall of the cabin were mounted the antlers of a moose that she'd shot one hungry winter. "Gave us a month of stews, the grand old fellow," she remembered fondly.

Later she took us into her cabin, where we washed our hands at the kitchen pump. Then she made tea and poured it from a china pot without spilling a drop. There was a silver spoon for the sugar and oatmeal cookies on a china plate. On the table's white linen cloth stood a vase of sweet williams and roses. Even my mother could not have found fault with Mrs. O'Neill's afternoon tea—it was most ladylike. But what would Mother have said about digging root cellars and shooting moose?

"Mr. O'Neill, God rest him, passed on thirty years ago," Mrs. O'Neill told me over tea. "Did I want to return alone to the old country? I did not! I raised three children in this place and good 'uns they are, too. In winter, I snowshoe to the store for mail and food."

I followed her bright glance. There, behind the door, stood a pair of snowshoes: deergut stretched over wooden frames. "Your Aunt Mary showed me how to make those," Mrs. O'Neill said. "She's a smart woman."

Aunt Mary smiled and said it was time to leave. I followed Feather to the door, wishing we could have stayed longer. Outside, Mrs. O'Neill caught my chin in her bony fingers and stared into my eyes. "You're full of the brightness," she said. "I don't need to see your palm to read your strong spirit. Don't let it be quenched, colleen. You listen to your heart."

In their pens, the goats bleated as we walked down the hill. I was silent, thinking about Mrs. O'Neill's words. Were they somehow an answer to what I'd asked my aunt about being a girl?

When we reached the road, my aunt clicked her tongue. "I've forgotten the tea," she said and gave Feather some coins. "You two run back to the store and fetch it for me."

As Feather and I reached the general store, four men passed in coarse pants and bright shirts. Their beards were woolly and their hats stained.

Outside, Mrs. O'Neill caught my chin in her bony fingers and stared into my eyes. "You're full of the brightness," she said.

Their huge boots clumped on the steps of the hotel as they entered the saloon.

"Curly Joe, you 'ave the money?" one of them called.

"Oui, oui, c'est vrai!" another replied, and a third man, an Indian with a long braid hanging over his shoulder, laughed.

"It's the Frenchmen, the loggers!" said Feather with excitement. "The log drive is coming through. We can get raisin pie!"

And off she ran towards the river while I raced after, trying to make sense of her words. Children lined the riverbank. And there was a steamboat, the *Islanda,* with a huge boom of squared timber she'd towed down the lake. On a platform, like a raft, stood four cabins, and from the roof of one smoke drifted.

"That's the cookhouse," said Feather. "The other cabins are where the men bunk."

She stared across the water at the cookhouse, licking her lips. "It's the best pie there is," she said. "And I know Mr. Ayotte, the cook. But usually the drive comes alongside the wharf. Today, it's too far out to get to."

"Dare you to run along the logs and get pie," said a voice behind us.

I spun around and there was Edwina, the girl who'd lost her hat overboard. Her freckles were scrunched up and she was laughing, her blond hair blowing in the wind.

"I dare you back. I double-dare you," I said quick as a flash. I was laughing, too.

"You first. I'll follow," she said.

I lowered myself off the wharf onto the closest timber. Although it was hewed flat along the top, it wasn't easy to stand on. It bobbed beneath my weight. Water slapped over it, making it wet. I unbuckled my shoes and threw them to Feather on the bank. A crowd of joking children gathered to watch. I ignored them. I straightened up and paid attention to the bouncing log.

I began to balance along it. This was not so hard; it was like walking the fence at home. Except that the fence held still and wasn't wet.

Now my feet were wet, too. I slid my toes forward carefully, letting them grip like cat's toes. It was too bad that I hadn't learned to swim yet; I was still learning how to float.

I couldn't look over my shoulder. "Are you coming, Edwina?" I called.

"Yes, of course."

I reached the end of the timber and looked at the narrow band of water that lay between it and the next one. Then I jumped, just a small jump, enough to get me over. The new timber sank beneath my weight and my feet slid. A splinter pierced like a needle, but I ignored the pain. I waved my arms and found my balance again. I didn't dare look back to shore or ahead to the cook's shanty. I smelled the pie, though. It was a warm, dark brown, sweet smell. My mouth watered.

I jumped another timber and another.

"*Attention!* Stop!" a man shouted. The cook stood in the shanty door. "You girls go back to shore! *C'est dangereux!*"

"Please, we'd like some raisin pie!" called Edwina and the cook rolled his eyes. "Pie, *tout le monde* wants my pie," he muttered and disappeared inside. Edwina and I kept moving, and when Mr. Ayotte came out again, we were only two timbers away. He walked along the wood himself, with a slice of pie on a tin plate in each hand. "Sit. Eat," he said.

We sat on the wet logs and ate every raisin, every sweet crumb of pastry. The pie was as good as the ones that Bertha made at home in Toronto. I asked Mr. Ayotte for a slice for Feather, and he rolled his eyes again but fetched me one wrapped in brown paper. Feather would know that I was not just a dumb city slicker when she saw me balancing along with her piece of pie. She'd want to be my friend for sure.

We thanked Mr. Ayotte and began walking the timbers to shore. My legs were tired now, and my balance didn't seem as sure as before. I wobbled. I slid. My arms were like windmills. I almost fell. I gasped. Edwina jumped onto the timber I was standing on, and it twisted along its length like a wild horse. I flew towards the water on the outer side of the boom. Feather's pie soared from my grasp. Green light closed over my head, then darkness. I thrashed my arms. Was I really going to drown in sight of the children on shore?

When I came up, I opened my eyes and reached for the timber. It was difficult to grip. My fingers dug into its hard grain. Beside me, Edwina was in the water gripping the timber, too. Her blond hair was plastered to pale cheeks.

"I c-c-can't swim y-yet," she stuttered. "W-we're just l-learning at c-camp."

"Let's try to climb up," I said. I gripped the log and tried to pull myself onto it. The timber rolled towards us, ducking us under. I heaved my body up, but slid back with a splash. Edwina hauled herself up, ducking me under. She let go; her head disappeared. I hauled her to the surface, her legs kicking my knees under water. "Hold on!" I yelled and set her hand on the timber again.

My arms ached and my legs were cold. "What are we going to do?" I asked miserably. Edwina's blue eyes were stretched wide.

Suddenly, the timbers began to bounce. Water sloshed into my mouth. Along came a pair of men's boots, and Uncle Eddy's face bent over us. "By the gosh!" he said, and he pulled us out by the arms. Then he escorted us back to shore, me walking in front of him and Edwina behind as he held both our hands.

Above the lock, the steamboat *Empress* was docked and a crowd lined her rail, watching. The children on the bank parted to let us ashore. No one was laughing now. Uncle Eddy's eyes blazed.

"Are ye out of your daft heads, ye nincompoops?" he asked. "Ye canna swim, neither one of ye, but off ye go over the logs. For why?"

"I dared her," said Edwina.

"I dared her back," I said, squirming uncomfortably.

"Aye, 'tis as your father warned me," said Uncle Eddy. "Ye leap before ye look—"

"Edwina!" shrieked a voice, and through the crowd rushed a woman in a white dress.

"Church camp director. I have to go," Edwina said and turned away.

Uncle Eddy bent and stared me in the eyes. "If ye were a lad, I'd give ye a good thrashing," he said. "Though lad or lassie, 'tis all the same for brains. 'Tis not boy brains and girl brains the Good Lord hands out. 'Tis brains to keep you safe and alive in this world. Ye ken what I'm saying?"

"Yes, Uncle," I whispered.

His knuckles rapped my head. "Start using the brains the Lord gave ye. Now run home and dry off."

I ran. Feather ran beside me, her feet silent in beaded moccasins. At the back door, we stopped to catch our breath.

"I'm sorry about your pie. I think it sank," I panted.

Feather's eyes were wide. "I thought you were going to drown for sure," she said. "That's why I ran and fetched Father from the boat."

"Thank you, Feather," I said. I felt terrible: I'd done something stupid again. "Can you please help me with my swimming?" I asked humbly.

"Of course," she agreed. "You're the only city cousin I know. I can't let you go to the bottom like a soggy piece of pie."

Suddenly, we both began to giggle, leaning against the rough siding, clutching our stomachs and holding our hands over our mouths.

"Looks like you girls are having a good day," said Aunt Mary peacefully, swinging the back door open. "Come in for some lemonade."

CHAPTER N.º 5

Several days later, Uncle Eddy brought home a newspaper. He flattened it on the verandah table and showed us the headline: "Britain's Official Declaration of War against Germany."

It was August 4, 1914, and a beautiful day. But a long shadow seemed to touch the pages as we read.

"Bang, bang!" cried Matthew, pointing his arm like a rifle and then playing dead, rolling down the steps onto the grass.

Aunt Mary gave Uncle Eddy a worried frown. "Will you have to fight?"

He shook his head. "They're only calling for volunteers. Those timbers you were on though, Millie, they're for the use of Her Majesty's Navy."

It was strange to imagine those timbers, smelling of lake and sap, being shipped across the Atlantic Ocean. Maybe a sailor would lay his hand on the exact spot where I had fallen off the wood.

"Will my father have to fight?" I asked.

"No. Some things may change," said Uncle Eddy, "but I don't think our families will be affected. This war will be over by Christmas."

In the weeks that followed, news of war seemed unimportant. Feather taught me to swim, and soon I could dive, too. I loved slipping beneath the ripples. Feather and Matthew taught me to catch sunfish with bread. We walked to Young's Point to watch steamboats lock through, and everyone in the family caught the *Stony Lake* to the Juniper Island Regatta. Edwina was there with her church camp, and we tied for third place in a swimming race. We cheered the ladies' canoe teams and bought sodas at the store to drink. By evening, everyone was sunburned. We steamed home between the islands while people sang "Moonlight on the Bay" and the regimental band played.

That night, as we climbed into bed, Aunt Mary told us that some of her family were camped at Eels Creek, and we'd visit them. Early next morning we loaded her canoe with food: pies, side bacon, beans, sugar and tea, fresh bread. We wedged folded blankets around the food.

"Safe journey," said Uncle Eddy, casting us off. Feather paddled in the bow and Aunt Mary in the stern, while I sat between. At Young's Point, the canoe was loaded onto the steamboat *Islanda,* and Feather and I roamed the decks while steaming northeast into Stony Lake, with its pink rocky islands and white pines. At a place called Crowe's Landing, the steamer tied to the wharf in front of the Bellvidere Hotel. Aunt Mary's canoe was set into the water again; we paddled across the lake to the northern shore.

On a point, beside the mouth of Eel's Creek, stood pale canvas tents. Canoes lay on the shore. Dogs barked as we paddled closer, but small Indian children watched in silence. Their cotton clothes were decorated with beads, and the tallest boy wore an owl's feather in his braided hair. When they ran into the trees, their feet were silent in moccasins.

We followed Aunt Mary up the trail to where her sister, Jane Two Stars, bent over a fire, roasting a plump porcupine. The sisters hugged, then sat to talk. I hadn't heard Aunt Mary use her own language before.

We spent a week in the camp. On the first morning, my aunt led us through the trees to where the men were building something. "This is a special small canoe," she explained. "It's for you, Millie."

"For me?" I stared in surprise at the curved wooden frame that the men had bent. Huge sheets of birchbark were curled over it and held in place with stakes.

"I don't even know how to paddle properly," I said.

"I will teach you," said my aunt with a gentle smile.

I could hardly believe that all the men's work was for me. I'd never owned anything as wonderful as this canoe would eventually be. "I show you," said Joseph, the son of Jane Two Stars. "This wood inside your canoe? Maple. And these rocks keep it bent while we work. Wood for nails."

He held out his palm filled with wooden pegs that had been whittled with a knife.

"Everyone, men and women, work on canoe," said Joseph. One of the women's jobs was sewing the sheets of birchbark together, using bone needles. For thread they used white spruce roots. Jane Two Stars let me take a turn—it was hard to push the tough roots through the bark. My fingers grew sore but I persevered.

"At home, I hate sewing," I told Feather. "Hems for handkerchiefs." I rolled my eyes and

Feather smiled. Sewing a canoe—a canoe for *me*—was different. It felt important.

The next day, we walked in the forest looking for spruce gum to scrape from the trees. While we searched, Aunt Mary and Jane Two Stars and her cousin showed me things. I saw where a cougar had sharpened its claws, where a raccoon had nested, where an owl had eaten a mouse. A snake had left a path in the wet leaves, and a skunk's footprints marked soft soil. The women knew the names of the plants; which ones to eat and which to make medicine from. After a day, I understood that Indians knew all about things my city neighbours had never heard of. I was filled with admiration.

The spruce gum was mixed with bear grease and charcoal. This sticky mixture was smeared onto the seams of my canoe, to make them watertight. Finally, Jane's husband, William, told me it was time to decorate my canoe. "What would you like?" he asked, heating a stick in the fire.

"Umm . . . a beaver," I said.

"Good. Beavers are like us," he said. "They work together, all family, to build lodges."

"And they swim, too," I said. "I love swimming!"

William smiled and pulled the stick from the fire. With its glowing tip, he burned a picture of a beaver on the bow of my canoe, and then added a north star. "So you never be lost on life's river," he said. "Your spirit finds home."

"This canoe is ready for water," said Joseph, and I nodded in delight.

"Wait," William said. "I tell you things. This canoe built with the Creator's gifts to his children: bear fat, maple wood, spruce root, birchbark. You remember today, Millie. Today is a good place to start loving the earth and all the Creator's gifts and all His children."

I nodded solemnly. It felt like being in church, with green leaves trembling overhead. William's voice was like the voice of the preacher at home in Toronto. He laid a hand on my shoulder. "Your canoe is ready," he said.

Joseph carried it to the water. It floated lightly as a leaf. It was beautiful, with its curving lines and pointed bow and stern. Jane Two Stars handed me a new carved paddle, and Aunt Mary climbed into her own canoe. "It's time to learn to paddle," she said. "We're going up the river."

I followed in my canoe, and Feather followed in one borrowed from her cousins. For three days, we paddled up and down the river between rocky banks and maples and dark cedars. The smell of the forest mingled with the smell of running water. Foam swirled below the rapids. A fish eagle cried, soaring overhead. My aunt showed me how to send the canoe in one direction or another, to shoot forward in a straight line, to turn quickly, to stop, to come sideways against the bank. She taught me to hold the canoe steady against the current's flow and to shoot through whitewater and sharp rocks, guiding the canoe with flashing strokes. I had never worked so hard to learn, or felt so excited and alive. It was like magic, the way my canoe responded to me.

On the last day, we lit a fire and cooked a rabbit. Sitting on a warm rock, we ate with our fingers. I had blisters from paddling.

"So today you have learned to ride the river," said Aunt Mary as she drank her tea. Her strong fingers, which knew many skills, gripped her tin mug.

"An elder said that life is like a river—a river of time. We all have to journey it. We all have to accept its currents. And you, Millie and Feather, you have to ride the river as girls. You cannot change this. But there are things you can change. You can choose the direction for your life and learn the skills to paddle where you want to go. You can learn to survive the rapids. Don't fight the water—use it to carry you where you want."

These were many words coming from my quiet aunt. She drank the rest of her tea in silence. But after she'd drained the cup, she smiled and repeated what William had said: "This is a good day to start loving the Creator's gifts and His people. And to love yourselves, girls, because He made you, too."

"And Louisa May," I added.

Aunt Mary smiled again.

Right then, on the sheet of rock, I felt perfectly peaceful. It was the best day of my life.

CHAPTER 6

One afternoon Uncle Eddy came home from the steamer with a letter from my father. He read it aloud as we sat around the table before supper. My father wrote that since the outbreak of war, his shipyard was twice as busy as usual and that he was working long hours. He said that he was considering sailing to Britain and signing up as a naval engineer.

This news sank into me like a heavy stone. How could Father even think of leaving his family and going off to war across the ocean?

"Would he really do that?" I asked Uncle Eddy in a small voice.

Uncle shook his head thoughtfully. "He wants to feel he's doing his part," he said. "But cheer up, lass. Ye'll be seeing him soon. He's coming to fetch ye home next week."

I smiled, my heart skipping a beat with excitement. It would be wonderful to see Father.

The final week of my holiday passed quickly. On the last day, my aunt and uncle went for an excursion on the steamboat *Stony Lake,* but my cousins and I decided to stay home.

In the morning we fished while mist drifted by in gauzy veils. Frogs and fish splashed, a loon called. "The heartbroken maiden calls for her lover," I moaned, before bursting into giggles.

Matthew snorted with laugher. Feather's lips curled upwards.

"Sorry," she said, but her eyes stayed solemn. "It is a true story, you know, about Polly Cow. My grandmother paddled in the funeral procession."

I stared through the mist. Maybe there *was* a spirit on the island, the gentle spirit of a girl who'd done no harm. Maybe it was her spirit we felt when the wind sighed at the edges of the mist— or her voice we heard when birds sang at dawn. Nothing on the lake seemed scary anymore.

At noon we paddled to a picnic place. I lit a fire using dried grass and small twigs, the way Aunt Mary had taught me. I even gutted the pickerel we'd caught, using Matthew's knife. We cooked them over the flames and they melted on our tongues.

Afterwards we paddled home so that I could pack. I looked at the three dresses I hadn't worn all summer. One was raspberry pink, the closest thing I owned to lavender. I shook the creases out.

"You can have this," I told Feather. "And these ribbons, too. I have plenty more at home."

"Are you sure? Thanks!" Feather slipped the dress over her shift. She knotted the ribbons into her hair, not just the pink ones but all of them, so that they hung down her back in a bright rainbow. My mother would've been amazed by such a hairstyle. Feather twirled before the mirror in her parents' room. Her dark skin looked beautiful against the pink fabric.

"Are you happy to be going home?" she asked.

"I'll miss our swimming."

And it was true, I would. But at the same time, I wanted to taste Bertha's ham, smell the milky-powder smell of Louisa May, hear my mother sing when I practised the piano. On the journey home, I'd tell my father about making my canoe, and about how Aunt Mary would keep it safe so that I could paddle it when I visited again next summer.

"I'll miss our swimming, too," Feather said, standing still with her back to the mirror. I could feel the friendship in her deep, soft eyes.

"Maybe you could visit me sometime in the city," I suggested.

Feather looked doubtful about this; perhaps she knew she'd feel as out of place there as a fish out of water. "Well, I'll write to you anyway," I reassured her.

"Yes," she said eagerly. "And I'll write back."

"Deal," I said, the way that Tommy did when we swapped marbles. Then we went out and lay in the hammock together, reading each other poems from Aunt Mary's copy of Longfellow.

In the evening, we canoed to Young's Point and bought barley sugar in the store. Matthew stayed to watch men playing euchre. Feather went to visit her friend Rose, who lived nearby, but I decided to go for a paddle. I wanted to spend my last hour on the lake in my beautiful canoe.

I paddled north towards Clear Lake, following the eastern shore. Slender birches crowded the edge. A mallard duck quacked among the lilies. When the sun set, the water gleamed golden and pink. Soon the *Stony Lake* would return with my aunt and uncle, and soon I would have to paddle back. I glanced north to see if the steamboat was in sight. It wasn't, but I noticed something else.

The lighthouse on the point was dark.

This lighthouse, on the western shore of Clear Lake, was cared for by old Finn. Every night at dusk, he rowed up the lake to the lighthouse and polished the glass with a rag. He poured oil into the lamp, trimmed the wick, and lit it. Its yellow beam helped boats enter the treacherous narrows north of Young's Point. In the village, they called it Finn's Light—and old Finn never forgot to light it.

But tonight the point was dark.

Something's happened, I thought. And soon the *Stony Lake* will steam home, crowded with passengers dancing to the band. The captain won't know about the light until too late.

I stared around but no other boats or people were in sight. Should I go ashore for help? No, that would take extra time. I would paddle across the lake myself and see what had happened.

With deep strokes I sent my canoe shooting across the dark ripples. I pretended I was in a regatta, struggling to win. My shoulders bent and swung over the paddle, and water chuckled under the bow.

*I wanted to spend my
last hour on the lake
in my beautiful canoe.*

I swept to the shore. My bow crunched on pebbles. I hauled the canoe out, scrambled over logs and rocks, then stood listening. It was silent and black beneath the cedars. For one moment I thought of ghosts, and then I took a deep breath.

"Finn?" I called. "Old Finn!"

Silence.

I stepped carefully along Finn's trail, which I could hardly see. Suddenly I tripped over something and my heart lurched. There was a moan. My blood pounded.

"Finn?" I asked.

I shook the body lying across the trail by the shoulders. Was it Finn? Was he ill—or injured? I shook him again and he moaned louder.

"The light," he said. "The light."

"Are you hurt?"

"Broke . . . my leg. Fell . . . over a root. Light the lamp. Hurry!"

Should I light the lamp first or get help for Finn? How long had he been lying in pain? Faintly, over the water, I heard the *oom-pah-pah* of a band. I ran to the shore and looked north-wards. There, drifting through the darkness, were the lights of the *Stony Lake*. Soon the captain would discover that the lighthouse was dark. Perhaps the steamboat would go aground on a rock or a reef, and the passengers would be in danger of drowning.

I sped back to the lighthouse and scrabbled for the latch. The door swung inwards to total black-ness. I peered in uncertainly. Then I reached one hand in and felt along the wall. There was a shelf. I felt a candle and a box of matches. The first match burned out but the second lit the candle. In the still air, I could hear the band playing clearly now. The tune was "Honeymoon Bay."

Holding the candle, I climbed the creaking steps to the top of the lighthouse. I set the candle on a ledge and lifted the glass carefully off the big lamp. With the rag lying on the shelf, I polished the glass clean. I looked for something to trim the wick with, but there was nothing. Old Finn must have carried a knife in his pocket. Should I fetch it? I stared through the dark window at the boat coming closer.

Light the lamp! screamed a voice in my head.

I struck a match and held it to the wick. Nothing happened. A second match. Nothing. The smoke made me cough. A third match burned more slowly and a flame crept through the wick, sucking up oil. *Please, please,* I begged it. The flame wavered in a draught of air, went out.

The door! I plunged downstairs and pulled the door shut, shutting out any draughts. Then I panted up again. This time the flame rose strongly, a bright sheet, and I set the glass over it. Its yellow light beamed into the night.

Now, help for Old Finn.

I blew out the candle and left it, then ran down the trail. When I shook Finn, he was silent. I dashed to my canoe just as the *Stony Lake* sailed past, her bright decks swirling with dancers. The thump of the band filled my ears. I jumped into my canoe and pushed off, angling the bow into the wash from the steamboat so that I wouldn't be swamped. Then I paddled behind it into Young's Point, where Uncle Eddy was the first man ashore.

"Old Finn needs help!" I cried, and soon a group of men left in a boat, rowing hard. We waited by the lock while I told my story to my aunt and uncle, and to Matthew and Feather, who'd come to meet the steamboat. Mrs. O'Neill stepped smartly down the gangplank in a beautiful gown of rose muslin.

"What's amiss?" she asked, and Uncle Eddy told her what had happened.

Her bright eyes sent me a look of approval. "That's the spirit, colleen," she said. "That's the strength in you. Don't you lose sight of it."

She patted my arm and gave each of us a peppermint to suck on while we waited.

Presently the men returned with Finn lying in the bottom of the boat. They lifted the old man out and laid him on a barnboard just as the doctor arrived. He covered Finn with a blanket, then followed as the men carried Finn home.

"He'll be fine now," Uncle Eddy said. "Thanks to ye, a brave, canny lass!"

"Edward," said a voice and we turned to see the captain of the steamboat. "Where's Miss Millie?" he asked. "Where's the girl who lit the lamp and saved Finn?"

He removed his peaked cap and shook my hand. "Miss Millie, you're my heroine. See you next summer?"

"Oh yes!" I agreed. "My canoe will be here for me. And my sister can come, too, when she's old enough!"

"We'll all be waiting for you," said the captain with a laugh, and beside him Mrs. O'Neill, Uncle Eddy, Aunt Mary, and my cousins all nodded and smiled.

"Yes, we'll be waiting," agreed Feather.

BIBLIOGRAPHY

Angus, James T. *A Respectable Ditch: The History of the Trent-Severn Waterway, 1833–1920*. Kingston: McGill-Queen's University Press, 1988.

Bow, Jane. *At the Foot of the Rapids: The Story of Peterborough*. City of Peterborough, 2000.

"Cap'n Young—Last of the Steamboat Captains." *The Leader*, August 17, 1978.

Careless, J.M.S. *Toronto to 1918: An Illustrated History*. Toronto: James Lorimer & Co.,1984.

Craig, John. *By the Sound of Her Whistle.* Toronto: Peter Martin Associates, 1966.

Duff, Garth. *Hazy Days in Dummer*. Self-published, 1991.

Hooke, Katherine N. *From Campsite to Cottage: Early Stoney Lake*. Peterborough Historical Society, 1992.

Knox, Gregory. *Bellvidere: Fond Recollections of a Stony Lake Hotel*. Self-published, 1987.

Mallory, Enid. *Kawartha: Living on These Lakes*. Peterborough Publishing, 1991.

Nathaway, Nan. *Yesteryear at Young's Point*. Self-published, n.d.

Paterson, Murray. *The Golden Years of Yesterday*. Comrie Publications, n.d.

Stephenson, Gerald. *Peterborough Canoe*. Peterborough Historical Society, 1987.

Tatley, Richard. "Steamboating on the Kawarthas." Kawartha Heritage, Peterborough Historical Atlas Foundation, 1981.

Young, Aileen. *I Hear a Boat A-whistlin': My Stony Lake Memories*. Self-published, 1992.

Acknowledgement

The author wishes to acknowledge the childhood memories of Aileen Young of Young's Point, whose family built steamboats.

Dear Reader,

Did you enjoy reading this Our Canadian Girl
adventure? Write us and tell us what you think!
We'd love to hear about your favourite parts, which
characters you like best, and even whom else you'd
like to see stories about. Maybe you'd like to read
an adventure with one of Our Canadian Girls
that happened in your hometown—fifty, a
hundred years ago or more!

Send your letters to:
> Our Canadian Girl
> c/o Penguin Canada
> 10 Alcorn Avenue, Suite 300
> Toronto, ON M4V 3B2

Be sure to check your bookstore for more books in
the Our Canadian Girl series. There are some ready
for you right now, and more are on their way.

We look forward to hearing from you!

Sincerely,
> Barbara Berson
> PENGUIN GROUP (CANADA)

P.S. Don't forget to visit us online at
www.ourcanadiangirl.ca—there are some
other girls you should meet!

1608
Samuel de
Champlain
establishes
the first
fortified
trading post
at Quebec.

1759
The British
defeat the
French in
the Battle
of the
Plains of
Abraham.

1812
The United
States
declares war
against
Canada.

1845
The expedition of
Sir John Franklin
to the Arctic ends
when the ship is
frozen in the pack
ice; the fate of its
crew remains a
mystery.

1869
Louis Riel
leads his
Métis
followers in
the Red
River
Rebellion.

1871
British
Columbi
joins
Canada.

1755
The British
expel the
entire French
population
of Acadia
(today's
Maritime
provinces),
sending
them into
exile.

1776
The 13
Colonies
revolt
against
Britain, and
the Loyalists
flee to
Canada.

1784
Rachel

1837
Calling for
responsible
government, the
Patriotes, following
Louis-Joseph
Papineau, rebel in
Lower Canada;
William Lyon
Mackenzie leads the
uprising in Upper
Canada.

1867
New
Brunswick,
Nova Scotia
and the United
Province of
Canada come
together in
Confederation
to form the
Dominion of
Canada.

1870
Manitoba joins
Canada. The
Northwest
Territories
become an
official
territory of
Canada.

Timeline

1885
At Craigellachie, British Columbia, the last spike is driven to complete the building of the Canadian Pacific Railway.

1898
The Yukon Territory becomes an official territory of Canada.

1914
Britain declares war on Germany, and Canada, because of its ties to Britain, is at war too.

1918
As a result of the Wartime Elections Act, the women of Canada are given the right to vote in federal elections.

1945
World War II ends conclusively with the dropping of atomic bombs on Hiroshima and Nagasaki.

1873
Prince Edward Island joins Canada.

1896
Gold is discovered on Bonanza Creek, a tributary of the Klondike River.

1905
Alberta and Saskatchewan join Canada.

1917
In the Halifax harbour, two ships collide, causing an explosion that leaves more than 1,600 dead and 9,000 injured.

1939
Canada declares war on Germany seven days after war is declared by Britain and France.

1949
Newfoundland, under the leadership of Joey Smallwood, joins Canada.

1901
Keeley

1885
Marie-Claire

1914
Millie